Monsters!

Monsters!

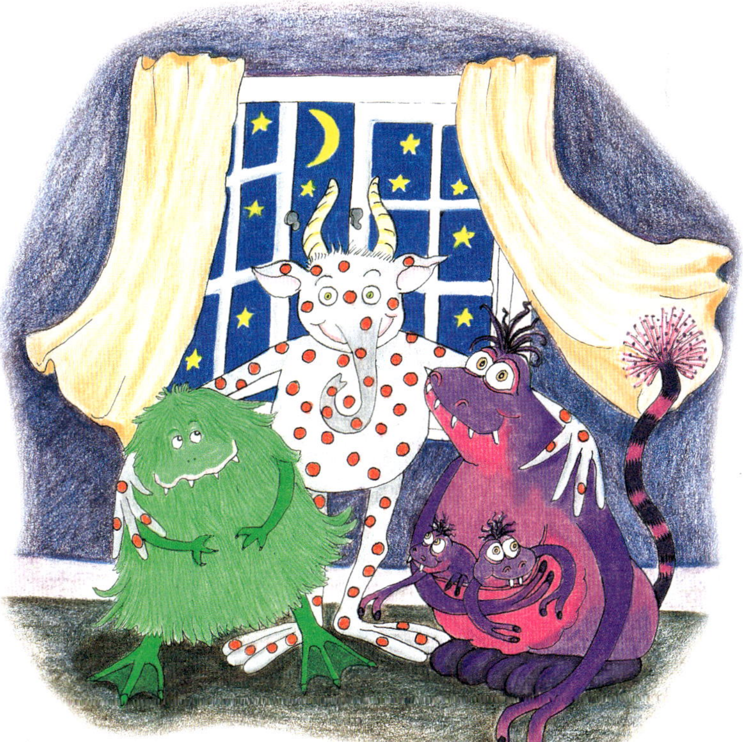

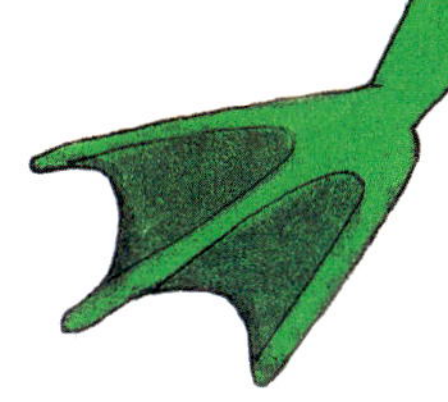

Monsters!

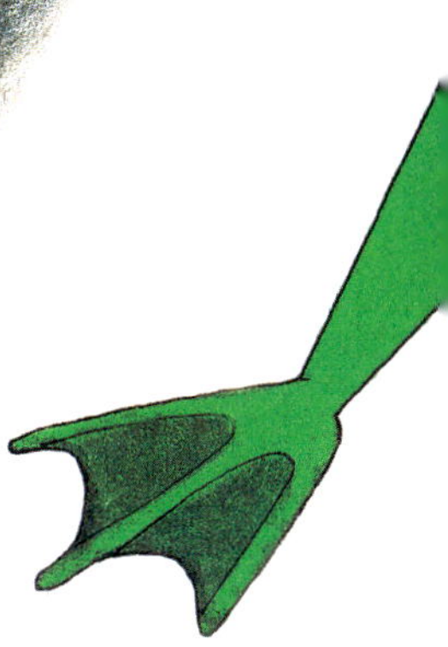

Monsters stomp

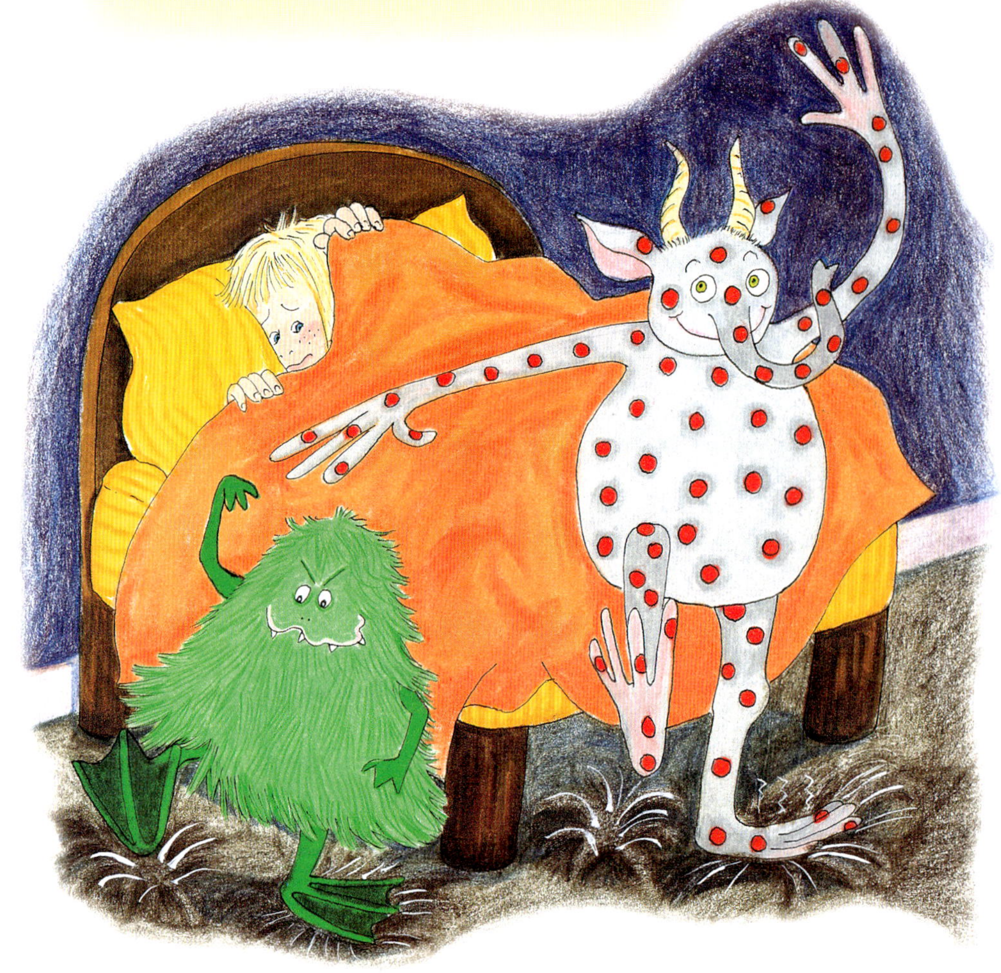

and stamp.

Monsters bash

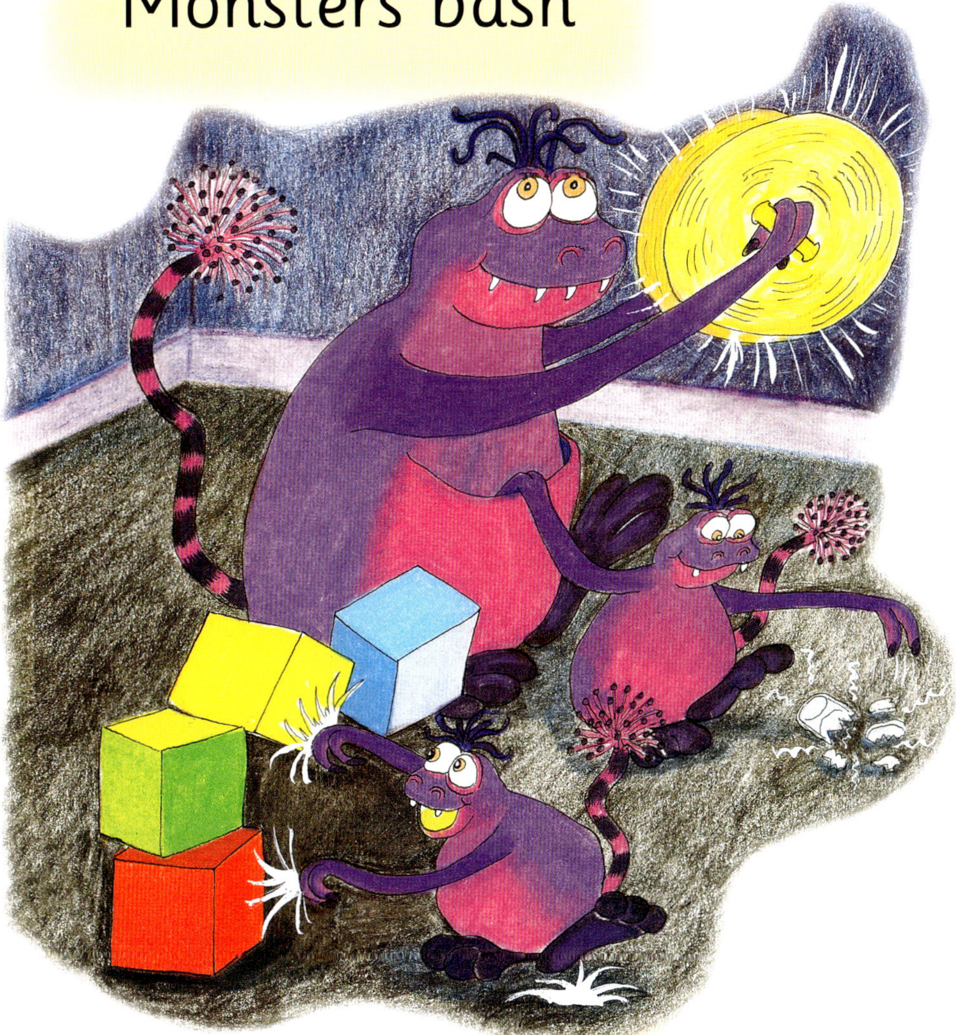

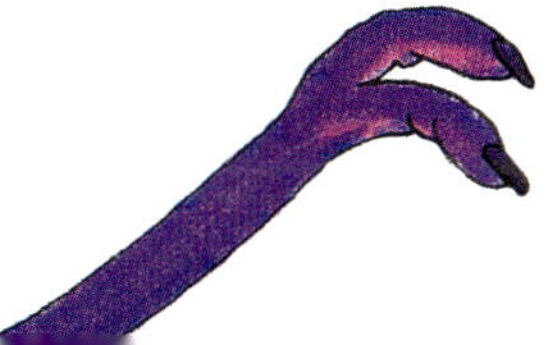

and crash.

Monsters flap

and clap.

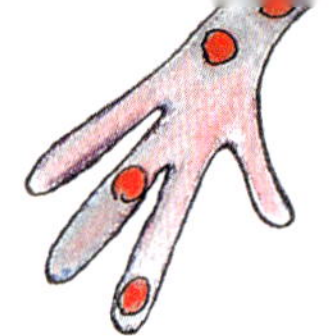

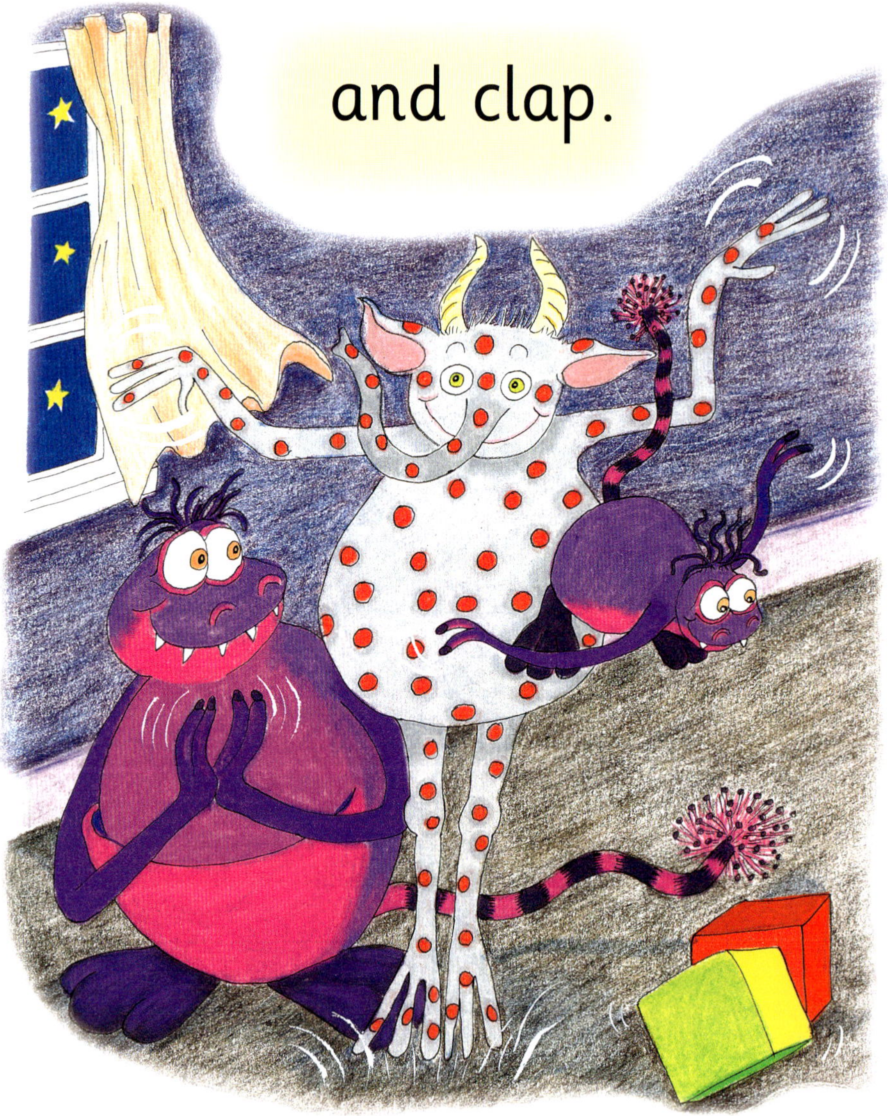

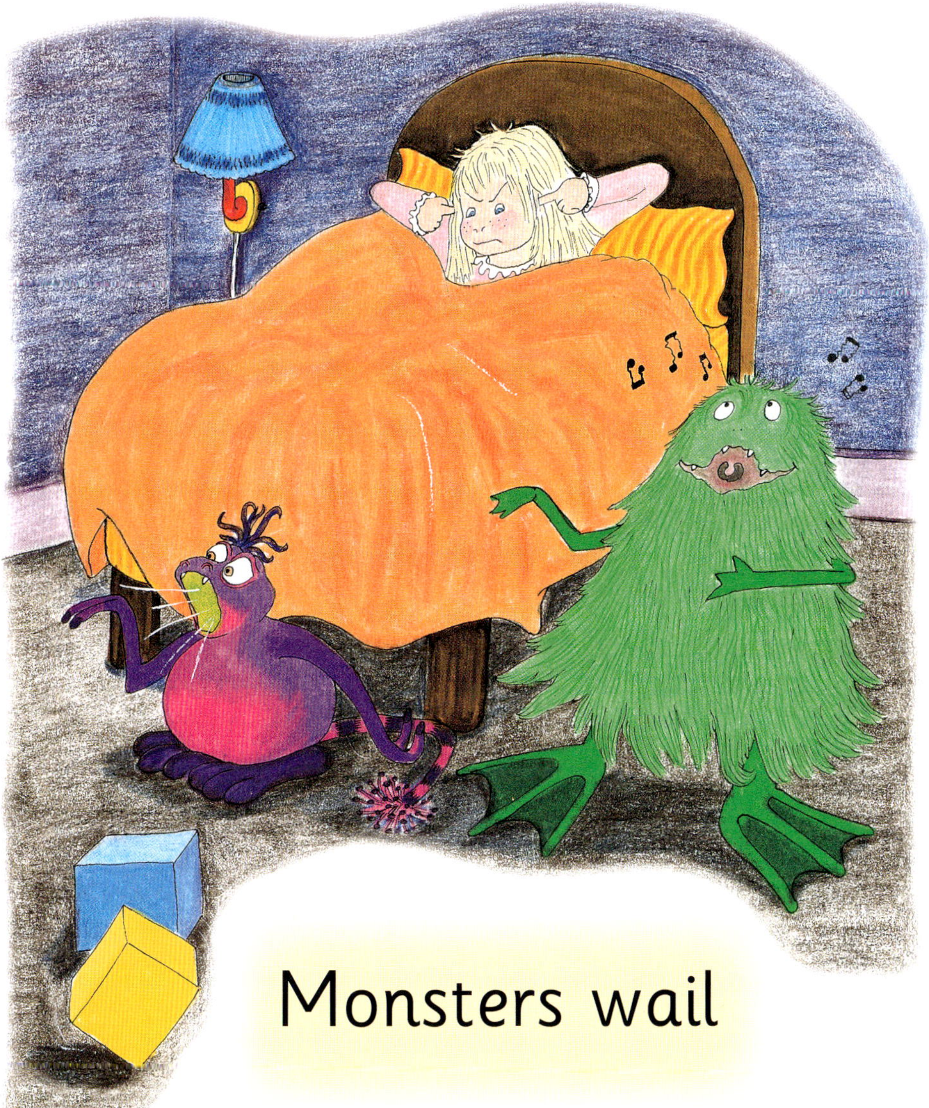

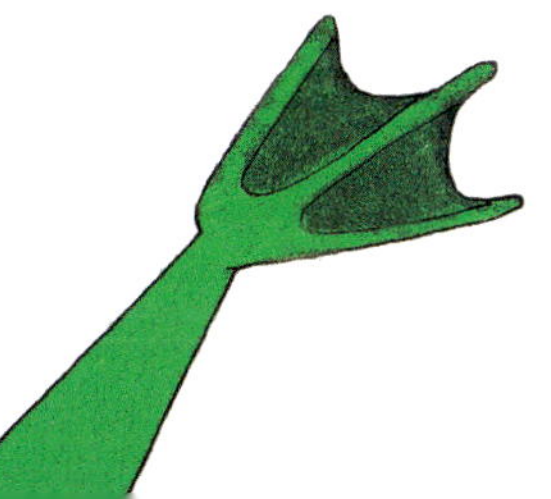

Monsters wail

and shout.

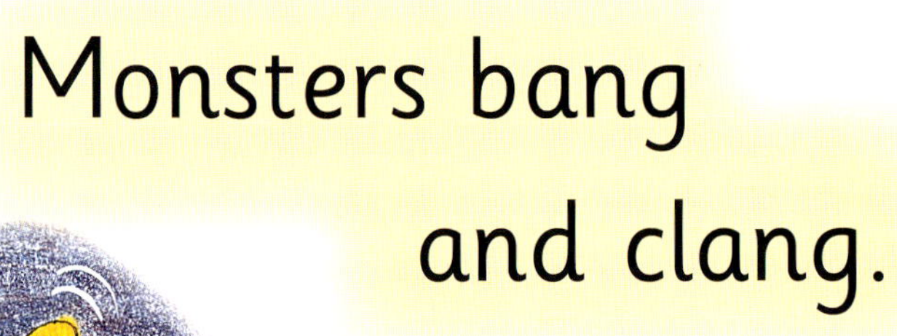

Monsters bang
and clang.

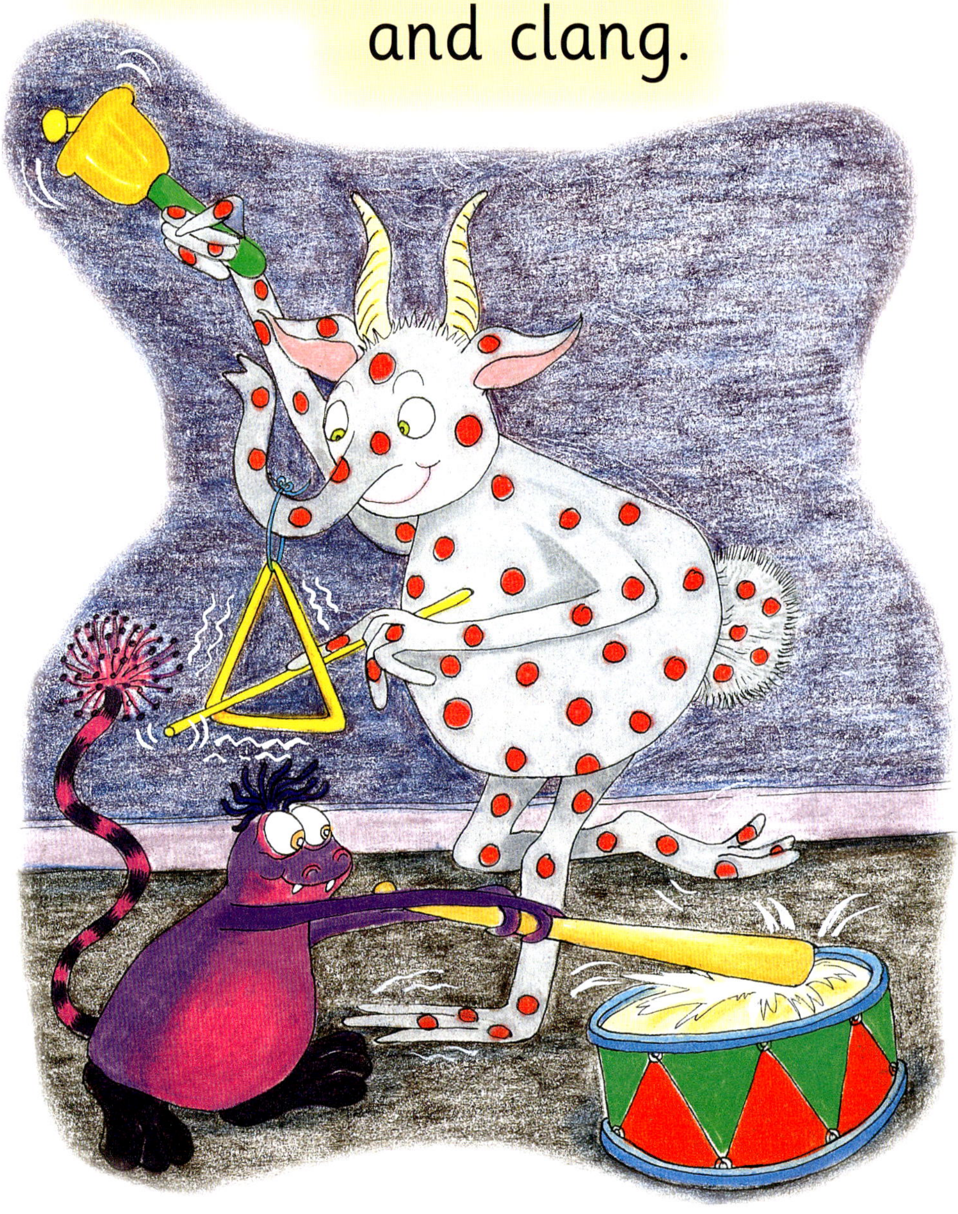

Monsters

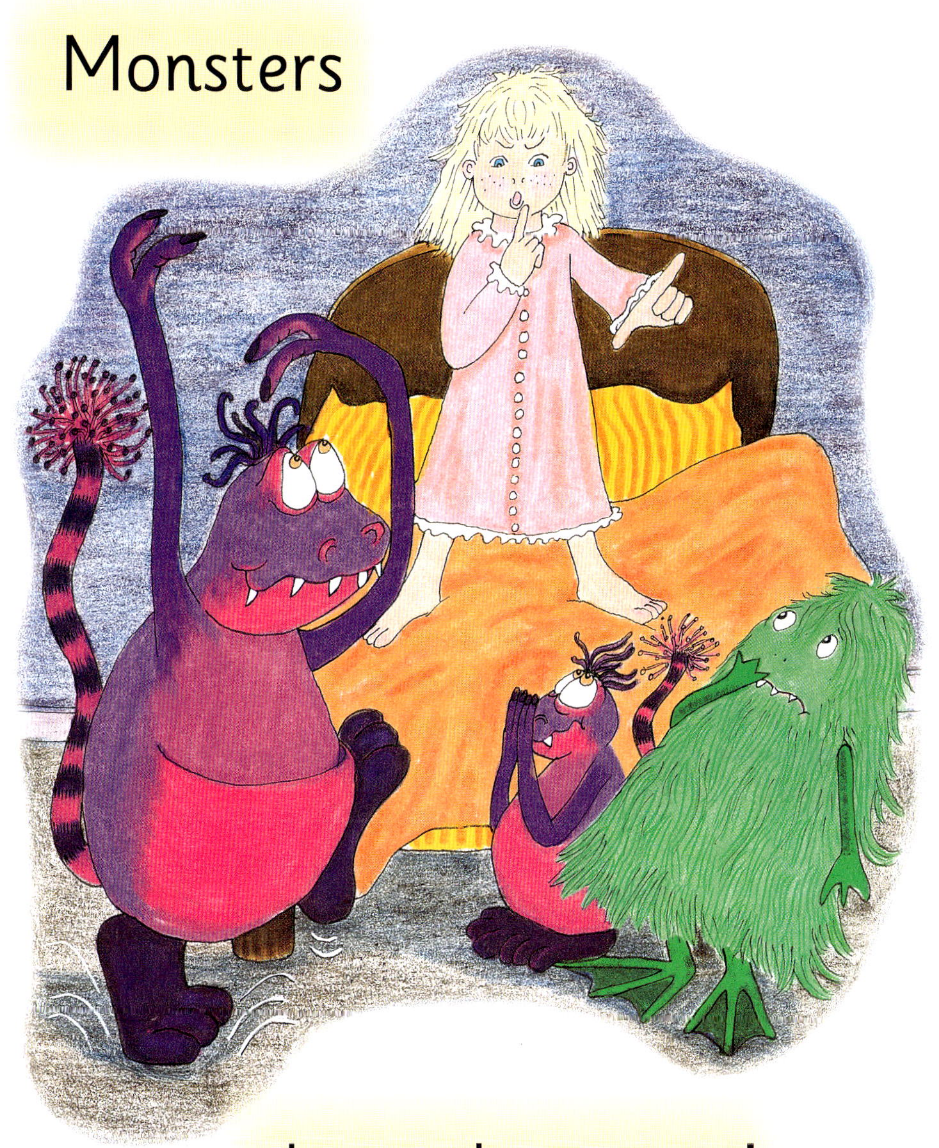

hop, then stop!

Monsters are sleeping.

Sh!

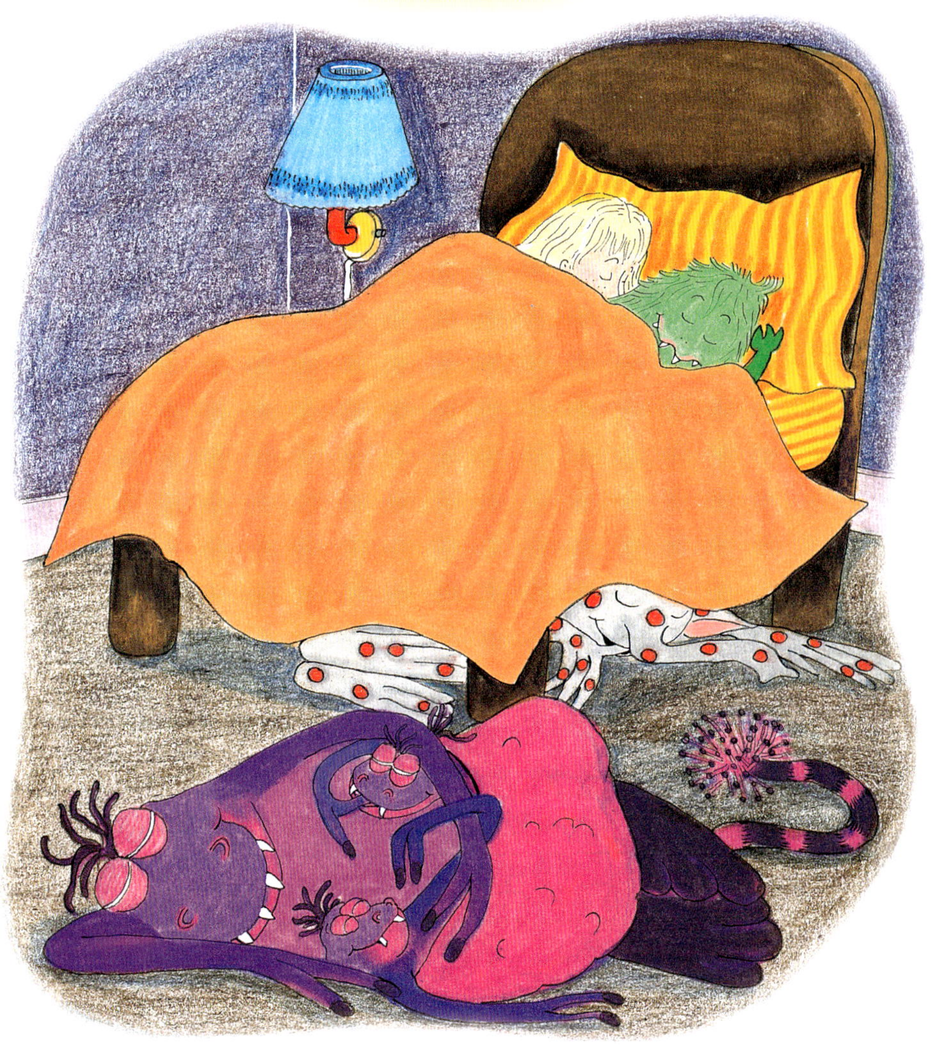